CROCO'NILE

ROY GERRARD

GOLLANCZ CHILDREN'S PAPERBACKS
LONDON

In ancient Egypt, long ago
Beside the River Nile,
A brother and a sister
Found a baby crocodile.

They fed it up on bread and dates,
And as it grew and grew,
It stayed the friend of Hamut
And his sister Nekatu.

Each morning when the girl and boy
Came down to have a swim,
Their trusty croc was waiting
For the fun they'd have with him.

One day they climbed aboard a boat
Whose crew had gone to dine,
And mischievously hid there
In amongst the jars of wine.

The naughty twosome stayed concealed
   Until the break of day,
By then their little village
   Was a hundred miles away.
Although the crew weren't really cross,
   They wondered what to do—
Returning was too risky
   For the floods were overdue,
And as the Nile would soon become
   A mass of waves and foam,
The stowaways must quickly
   Find a temporary home.

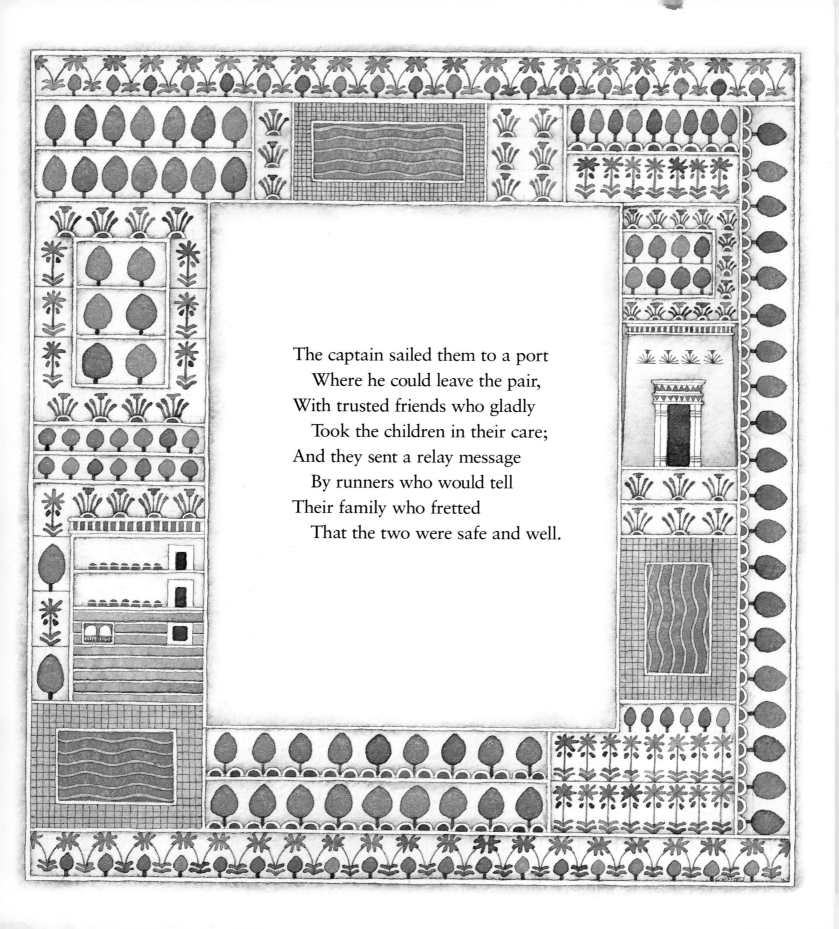

The captain sailed them to a port
　　Where he could leave the pair,
With trusted friends who gladly
　　Took the children in their care;
And they sent a relay message
　　By runners who would tell
Their family who fretted
　　That the two were safe and well.

They helped the children feel at home
By showing them the sights,
And pyramids that towered
To unprecedented heights.

Their guardian, who sculpted stone,
Taught Hamut with a will,
And soon he fashioned statues
With the most astounding skill.

And pretty soon, when Nekatu
　　Found she could paint and draw,
Egyptians gathered round her
　　To admire and gasp in awe.

The sculptor, keen to demonstrate
   The work these youngsters did,
Proposed that they should help him
   With the latest pyramid.
Deep in subterranean chambers
   Where sunlight never falls,
They carved and painted wonders
   Over all the passage walls.

The king came by to see the work
    And almost had a fit—
In all his royal life he'd
    Never seen the likes of it!
He asked them both to fabricate
    His dear queen's birthday treat,
A piece so rare and special
    That would make her day complete.

The children, who were thrilled to be
Commissioned by the king,
Began at once to fashion
An exquisite sort of thing.

And when at last their work was done,
   They had a bath and dressed,
And went to join the party
   At the palace, with the rest.

Now when the monarch's birthday gift
　　Was given to the queen,
She vowed it was the finest
　　That her royal eyes had seen,
And then the clever boy and girl
　　Were overcome with pride,
When ordered to be seated
　　At the table by her side.

Then these two junior geniuses
    Achieved enormous fame,
While managing to stay both
    Shy and modest, just the same.
But Fate held quite a shock in store
    Because, it's sad to say,
Some canny villains kidnapped
    Them, and carried them away!

Then brave Hamut and Nekatu
  Came home to scenes of joy,
And there were hugs and kisses
  For the long-lost girl and boy;
Then at the celebration feast
  The children praised their friend,
The constant crocodile who
  Gave this tale a happy end.

First published in Great Britain 1994
by Victor Gollancz
First Gollancz Children's Paperbacks edition published 1995
by Victor Gollancz
An imprint of the Cassell Group
Wellington House, 125 Strand, London WC2R 0BB

Copyright © Roy Gerrard 1994

The right of Roy Gerrard to be identified as author of this work has been asserted
by him in accordance with the Copyright, Designs and Patents Act, 1988.

A catalogue record for this book is available from the British Library

ISBN 0 575 06117 0

Printed in Belgium by Proost